CHRISTOPHER CHURCHMOUSE CLASSICS™

A STICKY MYSTERY

"Jealousy or selfish ambition are not God's kind of wisdom"
—James 3:15 (TLB).

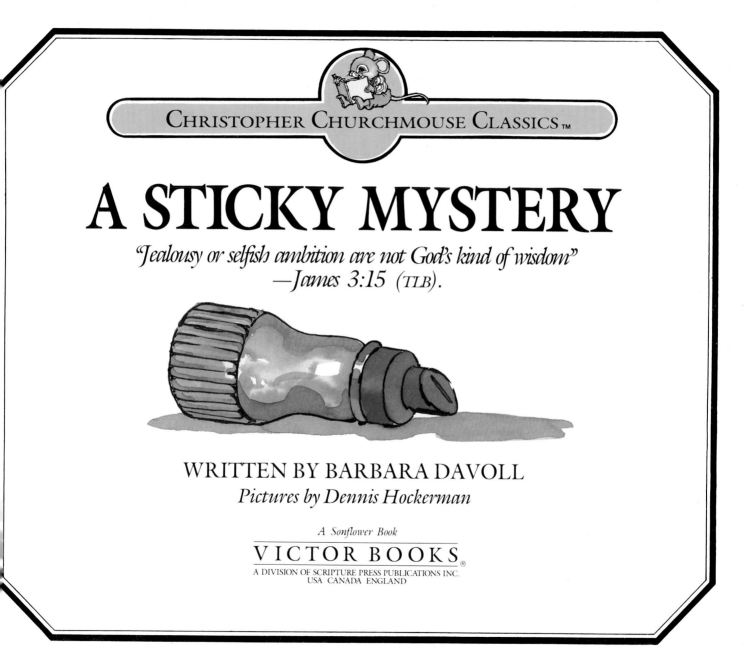

WRITTEN BY BARBARA DAVOLL
Pictures by Dennis Hockerman

A Sonflower Book

VICTOR BOOKS®
A DIVISION OF SCRIPTURE PRESS PUBLICATIONS INC.
USA CANADA ENGLAND

CHRISTOPHER CHURCHMOUSE CLASSICS

Saved by the Bell
The White Trail
A Sunday Surprise
The Potluck Supper
A Load of Trouble
Rainy Day Rescue
A Pack of Lies
The Shiny Red Sled
A Sticky Mystery
A Short Tail

Scripture quotations marked (TLB) are from *The Living Bible,* © 1971 Tyndale House Publishers, Wheaton, IL 60189. Used by permission.

ISBN: 0-89693-485-3

VICTOR BOOKS
A division of SP Publications, Inc.
Wheaton, IL 60187

A Word to Parents and Teachers

The Christopher Churchmouse Classics will please both the eyes and ears of children, and help them grow in the knowledge of God.

This book, *A Sticky Mystery,* one of the character-building stories in the series, is about jealousy.

"Jealousy or selfish ambition are not God's kind of wisdom"
—James 3:15 (TLB).

Through this story about Christopher, children will see a practical application of this Bible truth.

Use the Discussion Starters on page 24 to help children remember the story and the valuable lesson it teaches. Happy reading!

Christopher's Friend,

Barbara Davoll

Christopher Churchmouse and Freddie Fieldmouse came running out of school together onto the playground. It was recess time, and all the mice children were soon busy playing games.

"Hey, Chris!" called Freddie. "Let's go get a ball, and we'll play a game—just the two of us."

"OK. I'll go ask my cousin Sed if we can use the ball he's holding." Sed had been standing by himself, looking at Christopher and Freddie.

"Hey, Sed," yelled Christopher as he walked toward him. "Can I borrow your ball? Freddie and I want to play a game."

"I guess so." Sed shrugged his shoulders and bounced the ball to Chris.

Chris thanked Sed, and he and Freddie went off to invent a game with Sed's ball.

The two mice boys, Chris and Freddie, did almost everything together. They always walked to and from school together. They played together at recess. They played together after school. They even shared their lunches with each other.

5

When the recess bell rang, Christopher tossed Sed the ball and walked with Freddie to their classroom.

On the way they talked about what they were going to do after school. Suddenly, a brown blur slid around the corner, ran right in front of Freddie, and tripped him. Freddie fell facedown on the ground.

"What was that?" Freddie asked, looking up bewildered.

"I don't know. Are you OK?"

Christopher helped his friend up and dusted him off. "I think somebody meant to trip you, Freddie."

"Yeah, I think so too," said Freddie, continuing to brush himself off.

They didn't have any time to talk about it further because the bell rang to start class. They scooted into their seats just in time. Right after the bell rang, the teacher said in a stern voice, "Freddie Fieldmouse, please come to my desk."

Christopher looked up, surprised. Freddie was never in trouble with the teacher. What could the problem be? Christopher could see the teacher talking sternly with Freddie, and Freddie looked like he was about to cry.

8

At lunchtime, Freddie told Christopher what the teacher had said to him. "Remember when the teacher's drawer was glued shut a few days ago?"

"Yes," said Christopher. "It was kind of funny, wasn't it?"

"Well, it's not funny now! While we were at recess, the teacher found glue in my desk—the same kind of glue that was used to glue her drawer shut. I can't believe it!"

"Well, is it your glue?"

"No, of course not!"

"Someone's trying to get you in trouble, that's for sure." Christopher frowned.

"I guess so! Now I have to stay after school," said Freddie with disgust.

After school Christopher hung around the outside of the school building, watching as the mice left. Peeking around the corner, Chris saw a brown mouse looking in the window. He wished he could see better. As he watched carefully, Chris saw the mouse look in the window and then put his paw over his mouth and laugh. Christopher knew the mouse was laughing at Freddie, who was staying in after school.

When the mouse turned around, Christopher was so surprised he almost squeaked right out loud. It was his very own cousin Sed. Clapping his paw over his mouth to keep from making noise, Christopher stood frozen like a statue while Sed ran off.

Sed! I can't believe it, thought Christopher to himself. *Why would he want to hurt Freddie?*

11

Just then Freddie came running outside.

"Freddie, Freddie, I've solved the mystery! I know who's after you!" squeaked Christopher excitedly.

"You do?"

"Yes, but you'll never believe it, Freddie. It's my cousin Sed."

"Sed!" exclaimed Freddie. "I thought he was my friend!"

"So did I," said Christopher. "I don't understand this at all."

As soon as the two friends arrived at Christopher's house, Mama knew something was wrong.

"You both look so sad. What's wrong? Why don't you tell me about it?"

"Mama, you will never believe what happened today," began Christopher. He and Freddie told her the whole story of everything that had happened, including what Christopher had seen Sed do that afternoon.

When they finished their story, Mama said, "That is surprising. It's hard to believe Sed would do that."

"But Mama, why did he? He's my cousin and he's Freddie's good friend, or at least I thought so. I can't believe he doesn't like Freddie."

"What happened doesn't mean he doesn't like Freddie," said Mama. "I think Sed is suffering from jealousy."

"Jealousy?" said Freddie, leaning forward. "Is that some kind of sickness?"

"Well, no, not exactly," said Mama. "Jealousy is a bad feeling that you get inside when someone you like very much pays more attention to someone else."

"Oh," said Christopher. "You mean Sed may feel jealous inside because Freddie is my friend?"

"Yes," said Mama, "that's what I mean. Maybe he is jealous of your friendship with Freddie."

"Well, I don't know why that would be because Sed is my cousin and my good friend too. He has to know I like him."

"I know it seems that way," said Mama, "but Christopher, since Freddie has come to live in the church, who do you play with the most?"

14

"Well, ah—Freddie, I guess."

"And before Freddie came, who was your favorite playmate?"

"Sed," replied Christopher. "Sed has always been my favorite playmate."

"Don't you think," said Mama, "that maybe you and Freddie have shut Sed out and made him feel unwanted?"

"We didn't mean to," answered Christopher.

"No, we really didn't mean to," added Freddie.

"Do you invite him to play with you a lot?" said Mama.

"Well, no." Christopher couldn't look at Mama. He was remembering how he and Freddie had used Sed's ball that day but hadn't asked him to play with them.

16

"Do you see what I'm trying to say, Christopher?" asked Mama. "Maybe you've caused Sed to be jealous."

"Yes, I see what you mean, Mama," said Christopher quietly.

While Mama started cooking supper, the two friends went to Christopher's room to discuss the problem.

"I'm beginning to understand it all now," said Freddie. "But what can we do about this jealousy? Do we have to stop being friends?"

"I sure hope not," sighed Christopher.

"Do you think maybe if we are extra special nice to Sed and ask him to play with us and include him in everything, it would be better?" asked Freddie.

"Yes! I think maybe that would help," said Christopher. "Maybe you and I should talk to Sed."

"Talk to Sed? Not on your life. Not after what he's done to me!" said Freddie.

"Now, Freddie—listen. I mean, just tell him that we're sorry."

"Well, *he's* the one who should be sorry!" insisted Freddie.

"I know, but—but we kind of should be sorry too because we haven't included him in a lot of our playtimes, have we?" Chris reminded.

"No," said Freddie honestly.

"Then listen, let's go down to Sed's house tonight and talk to him."

Later that night the two mice boys knocked at Sed's door.

Chris spoke first. "H—hi, Sed. I wonder if Freddie and I could talk with you?"

"Um—talk?" asked Sed nervously.

"Yes—kind of a private talk," said Christopher.

"Well, I guess so," replied Sed.

Christopher thought Sed seemed a little worried. *Maybe he thinks we might punch him in the nose.*

They went to Sed's room and sat down on his bed. Christopher took a deep breath and spoke quickly, "We came to see you, Sed, because we know that we haven't been exactly right in just playing by ourselves all the time and not asking you to join us. We're sorry we've acted that way. We really like you, Sed, and we'd like you to play with us—and we want you to forgive us for not asking you to play with us before."

"Forgive you?" asked Sed in complete surprise.

"Yes," said Christopher. "Can we be friends again?"

"Sure," said the happy little mouse, sticking out his paw. "Sure—we can be friends."

Looking from Christopher to Freddie, Sed continued, "I'm sorry that I acted so mean toward you, Freddie."

"Aw, that's all right," said Freddie.

Sed continued quietly, "But I shouldn't have tripped you, and I shouldn't have told the teacher you glued her drawer shut when I did it." He looked down at his feet.

"*You* did it!" shrieked the two mice in unison.

"Yes, I did," answered Sed shamefully, "but I'll make it right, Freddie. I'll go to her tomorrow and tell her that you didn't do it and that I did."

Christopher looked at Freddie and somehow he just knew what his friend was thinking. "Why don't we go with you, Sed?" asked Christopher.

"Really? You'll both go with me?" exclaimed Sed. "That will be great!"

21

Later that week as the three mice boys were walking home from school, Christopher said, "You know, it's sure a lot more fun being friends than enemies."

"Yes," laughed Freddie, "but you have to admit it was fun solving the 'glue mystery.'"

"I don't know," giggled Sed. "It sure was a *sticky* one."

"I think we've learned a lot," said Christopher, laughing. And they had.

Together they had learned a lesson about jealousy which they wouldn't soon forget.

DISCUSSION STARTERS

1. What happened to Freddie that caused him to know someone was angry with him?
2. Who was angry with Freddie and Christopher?
3. What did Mama Churchmouse say she thought the problem was with Sed?
4. What had Christopher and Freddie been doing that hurt Sed and make him so upset?
5. Do you ever treat some of your friends as Christopher and Freddie treated Sed? How should you treat them instead?
6. What did Christopher and Freddie do to make things right between themselves and Sed?